One Night

NIGHTS SERIES BOOK ONE

A.M. SALINGER

COPYRIGHT

BOOKS BY A.M. SALINGER

NIGHTS

One Night - 1

The Escort - 2

Tokyo Heat - 3

Sweet Obsession - 4

Sweet Possession - 5

The Proposition - 6

Undisclosed - 7

Hush - 8

One Day - 9

Nights Series Short Story Collection

TWILIGHT FALLS

Alex - 1

Carter - 2

Hunter - 3

Wyatt - 4

Drake - 5

Tristan - 6

Miles - 7

CHAPTER ONE

WHAT THE HELL AM I DOING HERE?

Gabe Anderson scanned the crowded club in the mirror opposite the bar before looking down into his scotch with a self-deprecating smile. This had seemed like such a great idea an hour ago, when he'd been staring at an empty weekend in an even emptier apartment.

Saron was located in a side alley, a short walk from Shinjuku's main club strip. Despite its somewhat shady location, the place oozed style.

Gabe had hesitated when he'd seen the suited doorman guarding the entrance and wondered if access was by invitation only. He only knew of *Saron* from overhearing his clients mention it a few nights ago. From what he'd made of their excited conversation, it was *the* place to hang out in Shinjuku if you were of a particular sexual inclination.

The doorman had checked Gabe over for all of three seconds before wordlessly unclipping the rope from the stanchions framing the steel doors. He had obviously passed some kind of test, though what it was he didn't know.

Beyond a foyer with a cloakroom manned by a male attendant who looked like he'd walked straight out of a *GQ* shoot were a set of shallow steps leading to a wide, sunken floor.

Despite the butterflies churning his stomach, Gabe had stopped and stared appreciatively at the decor. As a consultant for one of Chicago's biggest design firms, he could tell how much money had gone into giving *Saron* its unique look. The club was drowned in deep reds, dark purples, and rich earth tones. Scattered across the oak floor were Brazilian cherry wood tables and armchairs boasting plush velvet upholstery and satin cushions. Discrete booths dotted the walls and afforded privacy to those who needed it, although the muted lighting provided enough of that as it was. A polished mahogany counter with wine-red leather and walnut stools ran the length of the bar on the right.

At the far end of the room, a woman in a black cocktail dress stood on a raised podium. She was crooning a song in a sultry, deep voice, her eyes closed and her glossy ruby lips glistening in the mellow spotlight. Behind her, cymbals vibrated gently, a piano tinkled, and a saxophone hummed, the sounds somehow rising above the voices of the men packing the place.

It was as he'd made his way to the bar that Gabe had realized why the doorman had let him in. From the looks of the club's patrons, *Saron* catered exclusively to an upscale clientele. He was willing to bet a week's wages none of the suits in the place cost less than five hundred dollars.

"Ah, fresh meat."

Gabe froze in the act of sitting on a barstool, his gaze swinging up to meet a pair of amused green eyes on the other side of the mahogany counter.

"Excuse me?" he said stiffly.

The bartender, a striking blond in a slate, silk tuxedo vest and crisp white shirt, flashed him a grin.

"I've not seen you around these parts before. What will it be?"

Gabe swallowed, wondering whether the man had seen straight through him and grasped the reason he had come to *Saron.*

"What will what be?" he mumbled, unable to mask the apprehension in his voice.

The bartender pursed his lips and observed him with a shrewd expression before leaning across the counter.

"Relax," he murmured in Gabe's left ear. "I can tell it's your first time in a place like this. If you keep up that deer-in-the-headlights look you've got painted across that pretty face of yours, you're gonna be a target for every sleaze ball in this club. And, trust me, they might be wearing thousand-dollar ensembles, but some of these assholes are nothing but dirty pigs in suits."

An involuntary bark of laughter left Gabe's lips at the mental image the bartender's words had conjured. The sound carried along the counter, drawing stares.

The knot of tension that had been sitting between Gabe's shoulder blades ever since he ventured into Shinjuku eased as he smiled at the bartender.

"I've never been called pretty before."

The guy winked.

"Trust me, you're the hottest thing on legs in this place right now. Besides me, of course."

Gabe chuckled and ordered a scotch, his confidence boosted by the compliment.

Two months had passed since he'd relocated to Tokyo from Chicago. When his bosses had sprung the offer on Gabe in early spring, the chance of a fresh start in a place void of the dark memories that had plagued him for eight years was too much of an attractive proposition for him to reject. He'd left Chicago with two suitcases and five crates full of books and artwork, the only things he had to show after a decade in the city.

Though he had been prepared for the culture shock, life in Tokyo had still come as a surprise, albeit an invigorating one. He had always had an interest in the country and its intoxicating mix of traditional and contemporary customs ever since he made his first business trip to the Japanese branch of the firm four years ago.

Luckily, his new position suited him to a T. He had thrown himself into his first assignment with his usual drive and passion, leading the team under him to make good on a project, one which his predecessor had only made a half-assed attempt to complete. He had delivered on time, on budget, and on schedule, despite the nearly impossible deadline. The crazy hours and weekends he had put in had not gone unnoticed, and the praise lavished on his team at the grand opening of their client's luxury hotel earlier that week was all the acknowledgment Gabe needed to realize he had made the right choice in moving to this city. The fact that the money he was making could easily afford him a two-bedroom condo in the exclusive neighborhood of Meguro didn't hurt, either.

Yet, despite having relocated thousands of miles to the other side of the world, his mind would not let go of the bite of his past. Which was why, when faced with the prospect of his first free weekend and the boxes he had yet to unpack, he had looked up *Saron's* location on the spur of the moment and decided to take a gamble.

He had promised himself this move would not be just a fresh start for his mind, but for his body, too. That he would start taking risks in his personal life again. That he would not let the bastard who had made it impossible for him to ever have a satisfying physical relationship win.

Fifteen minutes into his first drink and Gabe wondered whether he had made a bad choice. So far, Ethan, the bartender, had helped him field a burly, yakuza-looking type with tattoos up the side of his neck, three old men with sweaty palms and bald patches, and a couple of young guys who looked barely past the legal age of drinking.

With his lean build, dark hair, and blue eyes, Gabe knew he was an attractive prospect. Add in that he was a foreigner and he was coming to the conclusion that he had become a beeline for all the men in the bar who wanted to make a conquest out of the white guy – a white notch in the proverbial bedpost. They all wanted to fuck him or be fucked by him.

A cynical half-smile twisted his lips at that thought. If only they knew.

He raised a hand to the back of his neck and rubbed the warm spot that had been bothering him for a while. Something made him look up from his drink then – call it instinct or that subconscious voice that warns of imminent danger. Movement in the mirror opposite the bar caught his gaze. Or, more precisely, a lack of it.

Stormy gray eyes pierced him from the other end of the club. They locked on him, a beam of light in the gloom. Transfixing him. Immobilizing him.

Gabe's breath caught in his throat, every muscle in his body tightening in fight-or-flight mode.

The man sat apart from the crowd, alone at a table that could have accommodated three, a tumbler full of dark liquid clasped casually in his left hand. His red silk tie was crooked, as if he had slipped a finger through the knot to loosen it. The top two buttons on his white shirt were open, revealing tan skin covering toned muscles and a hint of curls.

Gabe couldn't tell whether his hair was dark brown or dirty blond. It was hard to say in the dim light. What wasn't hard to see were the subtle and not-so-subtle stares the other men in the bar were giving the stranger.

With his stubbled face, smoldering looks, and what appeared to be an incredibly ripped body beneath a custom-tailored charcoal suit, the man looked like a king sitting on a throne, commanding a roomful of servants. Servants who appeared more than willing to either get fucked by him or fuck him if he so much as lifted his little finger.

And a man like that would not have to ask twice.

Envy and irritation flashed through Gabe at that thought, shattering the spell he found himself under. He broke eye contact, shocked by the feelings suddenly flooding him, and glared at his half-empty glass. It seemed to mock him, as if it were a reflection of his own life. A half-empty, broken shell. Incapable of touching someone or to be touched.

Gabe lifted the glass and downed the rest of the drink with an angry flick of his wrist. Fire singed his throat. He welcomed the burning sensation, hoping it would calm the pounding in his chest and the tightness in his belly and groin that told him his body had reacted to the stranger.

A full glass of scotch appeared next to his empty tumbler.

Gabe looked up at Ethan, puzzled.

A remorseful grimace flashed across the bartender's face. "Looks like we're no longer the two hottest bastards in this joint. Here, compliments of the King."

Gabe stared at the drink before slowly looking over his shoulder, his pulse picking up speed.

Gray Eyes raised his glass in a toast. A teasing smile played on his sculptured lips before he knocked back his drink.

You're kidding me.

Gabe tried to block out the heated tingle running across his skin at the stranger's cocky smirk and the way his powerful throat muscles worked when he swallowed. He turned to Ethan.

"That's his *actual* name?"

Ethan grunted. "Well, no. But the asshole sure acts like one."

There was movement in the mirror opposite Gabe.

CHAPTER TWO

CAM RAN A HAND THROUGH HIS HAIR AND CAUGHT A whiff of the cloying perfume that had been giving him a pounding headache the entire afternoon. He grimaced, took a sip of his drink, and tugged at the knot in his tie. The familiar scotch scorched his throat, sending a wave of welcomed warmth through his stiff body. He loosened a couple of buttons and sat back in the chair, closing his eyes for a moment while he willed the lingering smell and his tension away.

Though he loved his job, being an asset manager for one of the biggest investment firms in Asia often involved dealing with troublesome clients. The one that afternoon had proven more challenging than most. Not that Cam had let that deter him from securing the deal.

The woman, a wealthy widow with more millions than she knew what to do with, had come on to him from the moment he'd sat on the couch in the expensive hotel room where she had insisted their meeting be held. Her fingers and red nails had touched his shoulders and thighs whenever she laughed, while her thick, sweet perfume had choked the air around him, bringing on a rare migraine.

Though he was bisexual and could bed a woman as easily as he could a man, Cam made it a rule to never mix business with pleasure, especially in this kind of high-powered transaction. Besides, he would never do anything to compromise his hard-earned reputation. It was the reason he had been headhunted for this job in the first place; he was the only candidate the firm had been willing to wait over a year for while he made up his mind whether or not to accept their offer. Though it had never been Cam's intention to keep them hanging for that long, the thrill of power it had given him was compelling validation for everything he had achieved since he turned fifteen.

Bar his closest friend, no one in the circles he ran in knew of his trailer-trash background. He'd be willing to bet that the woman who had so evidently wanted him to bed her that afternoon would run a mile in the other direction if she knew of his heroin-addicted single mother and the institutions where he'd spent his early teens after she died from an overdose, leaving him the clothes on his back and fifty dollars in change.

While the widow openly flirted with him, her secretary had watched on, an apologetic wince occasionally dancing across her face. Cam had smiled at her at one point and masked his amusement when she squirmed in her seat. She had been dressed in a rigid pantsuit, the stark gray color clashing with her fair skin and brown hair. Though she had come across as serious and mousy, he could tell from the way she'd crossed and uncrossed her legs and her faint musky scent that she'd been aroused. If it hadn't been for the throbbing pain in his skull, he would have invited her for a quick drink and given her the screaming orgasm she so clearly deserved.

Cam had always had a soft spot for the quiet ones. More often than not, they were the sexual partners who surprised him the most in the bedroom, their sensuality and willingness to experiment giving him some of the best climaxes he had ever had, be they male or female.

He'd come straight to *Saron* from the hotel, the need for a drink and the company of his best friend high on his agenda for the night. Though the club was as busy and noisy as he'd expected it to be on a Friday night, he did not mind the hustle and bustle. *Saron* had always been an oasis of calm in Cam's hectic life and the one place bar his condo where he could truly relax.

To his chagrin, Joe wasn't in yet.

Though he owned *Saron* outright and had been making a sweet turnover for the last couple of years, Joe Cavendish had not completely given up on his former life as a high-end male escort and still accepted the odd offer from his ex-employer, the woman to whom he owed his current lifestyle in Tokyo and who had helped him escape the shady underworld of New York's sex clubs.

Cam had been stunned to see Joe when he'd walked into *Saron* eighteen months ago. The last time the pair had been in each other's company was the night they ran away from the children's home where they had been living. Meeting his old friend again twenty years later in the city he now called home had been a most welcome surprise for Cam, and they had fast rekindled the friendship that had kept them sane throughout their time together in the godawful place where they spent their early teenage years.

The fact that Joe was also bisexual had not shocked Cam. He'd always suspected Joe was, just as he himself had come to terms with his own sexual nature when he entered his twenties.

Besides being a haven, *Saron* was also the place Cam came to when he wanted to bed a man for the night. Relationships weren't his thing, nor were they Joe's. Short, hot, wicked sex had always been their style, although things looked likely to change soon for his best friend.

Though he could have his pick of his clientele, Joe also made it a point not to mix business with pleasure, a fact that was causing Ethan Skye, his most successful bartender, to be as ornery as a shaken wasp nest. Cam had watched the rising sexual tension between Joe and Ethan for some eight months now and was willing to bet a month's wages they would be shacked up by the time the clock struck midnight at the New Year.

There was no doubt in Cam's mind that the brooding club owner and the feisty bartender suited each other well, and he knew it was the fear of entering a potentially long-term relationship that had Joe currently fleeing for his life.

Cam smiled drily into his drink as he considered whether to have a talk with Joe before Ethan blew a proverbial gasket and attacked him. He was hardly in a position to play the role of agony aunt, considering the lack of romantic relationships in his own life.

Unlike Joe and Ethan, falling in love was something Cam never intended to do. He would never make himself that vulnerable for another person again. Not since he'd walked into the bathroom of the trailer where he had been born and found his mother dying on the floor in her own vomit.

Although she had been far from perfect, she was the only relative he had had in the world and the only person who had ever showed him any love, however scarce those moments had been. The day his mother cruelly abandoned him was the day Cam swore he would never allow himself to care for another person so deeply for as long as he lived.

The age-old pain stabbed through him as he relived the moment of her death once more, the horrible sense of betrayal he had suffered that day threatening to drag him down into an abyss of bitter memories. Despite the success he had achieved and the wealth he had accumulated since he fled the children's home and decided to carve out a future that would never see him having to beg for food ever again, he didn't need a psych report to concede that the scars of his past had still not healed.

Cam took another sip of his drink and pushed away the dark thoughts clouding his mind, determined not to let them ruin his night. A commotion ahead and to the right drew his gaze, distracting him.

A man was making his way toward the bar, his passage marked by swiveling heads and stares. Cam caught glimpses of a dark head and a navy blue suit, the outfit hugging a toned build and long legs. He frowned into his drink and swirled the amber liquid around before swallowing another mouthful.

He wasn't interested in a bed partner tonight.

Cam glanced at his watch and was wondering how much longer Joe would be, when a throaty male laugh reached his ears. The sound raised the hairs on his nape and sent a hot prickle straight to his groin. Cam looked up just as a gap appeared in the crowd and finally saw him.

The tension that had slipped away in the past quarter of an hour returned tenfold. Cam's whole body tightened, his cock hardening in a matter of seconds.

The guy sitting at the bar talking to Ethan was the most stunningly sexy thing he had ever seen in his life. Cam's heart stuttered as he hungrily took in every single detail of the stranger through the breach in the throng of men milling the club and the mirror opposite the bar.

Tall, lean, with straight dark hair and an arresting ice-blue gaze, the guy wore an easy smile, the laughter lines at the corners of his eyes wrinkling slightly as he responded to the bartender's light banter. Though he seemed relaxed, Cam could tell he was tense from the rigid lines of his shoulders.

He found his gaze following the contours of the

stranger's body, from the elegant way he held himself on the barstool to the sensuous line of his spine and his sweet, firm backside. All thoughts of spending the night chilling out with Joe fled Cam's mind. A shudder raced through him when he glimpsed the taut muscles moving sensuously beneath the fabric of the stranger's trousers as the latter shifted position on the barstool. Cam wondered how those thighs would feel wrapped around his waist while he fucked that impossibly fine-looking ass.

Would he scream or would he moan?

Cam couldn't wait to find out. And he knew he would. That this man would be writhing in pleasure beneath him at some point in the coming hours was an undeniable truth. No one had ever refused him.

He forced himself to stay put and watched curiously as several of the club's regulars approached the guy he intended to bed, only to be politely and resolutely rejected by him with Ethan's amused assistance. Cam caught the eye of a waiter and waved him over.

"What's he having?" He tilted his head toward the bar.

The waiter, a newbie, glanced nervously to where he indicated.

"Scotch on the rocks," he mumbled, ears flushing and eyes nervously taking in Cam's intimidating presence.

Cam's gaze locked on the blue-eyed man once more, his arousal straining uncomfortably against his pants.

"Make it a double," he ordered.

The waiter nodded and disappeared in the crowd.

The man at the bar reached up and rubbed the spot on the back of his neck Cam had been boring into for the last ten minutes. He stilled, his entire body freezing in the next instant. His head rose and he stared straight at Cam through the mirror. The ice-blue gaze flared. Awareness flashed across his gorgeous face as they gazed at one another for a timeless moment.

Cam's pulse accelerated, blood flooding his already rigid hard-on.

The man suddenly broke eye contact, a scowl darkening his features.

Cam blinked, stunned by an unexpected feeling of loss. Irritation darted through him with his next breath. His ire rose when he caught Ethan staring at him pointedly from behind the counter, his "keep-yourself-and-your-dick-away-from-my-new-buddy" expression plain to see. He poured Cam's order nonetheless and pushed the glass toward the stranger.

The man looked at it blankly before staring at Ethan. The bartender leaned over and murmured something. The stranger stiffened. He glanced at Cam over his shoulder, an incredulous expression on his face.

That's it.

Cam swallowed his displeasure, raised his glass in a mocking toast, and flashed a bold smile at the man at the bar before downing his drink. He adjusted his suit jacket to hide his arousal, rose, and headed across the floor.

CHAPTER THREE

Gabe saw the crowd parting behind him in the mirror, bodies moving aside hastily to make way for a formidable figure. Hairs rose on the back of his neck.

The gray-eyed king was walking leisurely toward him, his dark hair catching the light.

He stopped on Gabe's left and cocked an eyebrow at the man occupying the adjacent barstool. The latter mumbled something before slinking away into the crowd, face flushed.

Gabe wondered wildly if the newcomer had that effect on everyone.

The king propped himself on the seat.

"Double Scotch," he said, his laser stare on Ethan.

His voice was low, throaty. It danced down Gabe's spine, bringing a flash of torrid, filthy images to his mind.

It was a voice made for the bedroom. For hot, dirty-as-fuck sex.

The air between them swirled and thickened,

making it hard to breathe. Gabe inhaled shakily, startled by the feverish sensations flooding his chest as he stared at the man beside him through the mirror.

He had not expected this when he came to *Saron* tonight. Not expected his body to react in such a primal way to a man he had never met before, a complete stranger who had just bought him a drink, making his intentions all too clear.

Gabe steeled himself before turning his head and meeting the gray stare head-on, wondering if this man could give him what he so desperately wanted, if he could heal the wounds of that ungodly night eight years ago. Wondering whether he would return to his condo in Meguro a man able to have sex again or remain the empty, broken shell he had been for as long as he could remember.

All it took was one look into the gunmetal gaze watching him from a foot away for Gabe's fate to be sealed. He swallowed, his cock stirring.

Oh, fuck.

"I'm Cam. Cameron Sorvino," the man said. He offered his hand.

Gabe hesitated before shaking it, his heart drumming against his ribs. He wondered if the man next to him would hear the sound and detect the fine tremor in his fingers.

Cam's grip was firm and warm, his touch casual before he let go.

"Gabe Anderson," Gabe murmured. His hand burned from the brief contact, as if it'd been branded.

Cam's mouth lifted at the corner, his lips stretching

in a devastatingly sexy smile that made Gabe's pulse jump even higher and sent blood surging toward his groin.

I am SO screwed.

"Is that short for Gabriel?"

"No. Just plain old Gabe." Gabe winced inwardly. *Christ, I sound like a complete moron.*

Amusement flashed in Cam's eyes, as if he'd read Gabe's mind. "Can I take a sip?" He indicated the drink he'd ordered for Gabe before glancing across the mahogany counter. "The help is slow tonight."

Gabe dipped his chin in acquiescence.

"Yeah, well, that's 'cause the help is worried about the asshole preying on his new buddy," Ethan muttered.

"Says the guy who wanted me to bed him the moment he laid eyes on me," Cam tut-tutted. He took a mouthful of Gabe's scotch before sliding it back toward him.

Gabe found his gaze dropping to Cam's wet, full lips. He swallowed a groan and reached for the tumbler, gulping half of its contents as need speared through him. Embarrassment brought a flash of heat to his ears when he realized they'd just shared an indirect kiss.

"As if," Ethan scoffed. He handed Cam a fresh glass of scotch, a frown marring his brow. "My butthole would shut down in shock if your dick ever got close to it. I'd probably die from constipation."

Gabe choked, glad he'd already swallowed most of his drink.

Cam and Ethan stared at him, their expressions warming when he wiped his mouth with the back of his hand and laughed out loud.

"I'm sorry. That mental image is just—"

"Here, you missed a spot." Cam reached over and ran his thumb across the corner of Gabe's mouth, abruptly interrupting his train of thought.

Fire licked Gabe's skin. His breath hitched in his throat as he locked eyes with Cam. It took all his willpower to resist the urge to flick out his tongue and taste the man touching him.

The vivid picture the sudden impulse evoked struck Gabe like a bucket of ice-cold water. He turned from Cam, mortified by his wanton desire for the stranger next to him. His gaze dropped to his drink.

Maybe they were right. The men from that night. Maybe I'm as indecent as they thought I was.

His gut twisted, shame and remorse filling him in equal measure, cooling his arousal.

CAM LOWERED HIS HAND AND CASUALLY TOOK A SIP OF his drink, the pad of his thumb burning. He was stunned by the strength of the emotions swirling through him after touching Gabe.

He saw Gabe's knuckles whiten around his own glass and detected the faint color tainting his sculptured cheekbones in the mirror opposite the counter. He knew instinctively it wasn't just lust that had made this man flush. Though the sparks of attraction between them were so vivid he thought they would ignite the very air in the club, Cam sensed more than desire from the stranger sitting a foot from him. It was becoming clear to Cam that Gabe hadn't come to *Saron* to just pick up a bed partner for the night. Instead, he seemed to be a man conflicted, doubt darkening his beautiful face while his blue eyes expressed curiosity and sexual interest.

A flash of intuition darted through Cam then. Gabe had secrets of his own, dark ones by the looks of things.

This realization would normally have had Cam running a mile in the opposite direction. He didn't do emotional baggage. Yet he found himself rooted to the barstool, unable to distance himself from the alluring, mysterious man beside him. He wanted to know more.

"Are you visiting or do you live here?" Cam said, his tone light.

Gabe hesitated. "I moved here a couple of months back," he murmured.

"For work?"

Gabe nodded, his shoulders dropping slightly as he started to relax.

"Hey, what's with the twenty questions?" Ethan hissed. The bartender had returned from serving a couple of patrons further along the bar.

Cam cocked an eyebrow.

"It's called making conversation. Besides, this guy's a sitting target. If either of us leaves his side, he's gonna get attacked by half the assholes in this club."

Ethan grimaced. "That's true. They can smell fresh

meat from half a mile away." He narrowed his eyes. "Never mind that the biggest asshole in here is sitting next to him right now."

Gabe frowned. "Will you stop calling me that? And I'm a guy. I can protect myself."

"I don't think so, cupcake," Ethan drawled. "If I hadn't intervened earlier, that yakuza guy would be pounding your sweet ass somewhere in a back alley right now."

Delight filled Cam when Gabe soundlessly opened and closed his mouth, ears flushing even redder. He wondered if it was the "pounding" or the "sweet ass" making him blush so fiercely.

"What kind of crass bullshit are you spouting now?" someone said behind them.

&.

GABE STARTLED. HE TURNED TO LOOK AT THE intimidating man with dark hair and stubbled jaw who stopped next to Cam.

"Joe," Cam said, his tone relaxed and his lips curving into a welcoming smile.

Ethan eyed the newcomer up and down. His gaze turned accusing as it roamed the undone top buttons of the man's shirt and his expensive, casual gray-blue suit.

"Did you go to that place again?" the bartender said stiffly.

The stranger's hazel eyes narrowed. "That's none of your business."

A flush of color stained Ethan's cheeks. He poured another scotch on ice, slammed the glass on the counter, and strode away.

"Did he just flounce?" Cam muttered.

The stranger sighed. He picked up the drink, his gaze shifting from Ethan's disappearing back to Gabe.

"I apologize if my staff have been rude to you. I'm Joe Cavendish, the owner of *Saron*."

"Not at all," Gabe murmured, aware of the stares they were drawing.

Joe and Cam made for an impressive sight where they lounged at the bar. Compared to them, Gabe felt like an awkward, ugly duckling.

He chided himself for that cynical thought and indicated the club's interior with a tilt of his glass.

"I like the style of the place. Who designed it?"

Joe blinked, surprise flashing across his face for a moment.

"Damon & Tucker."

Pleasure and pride coursed through Gabe. He smiled faintly as he gazed around the club.

"I didn't know we took on projects like this."

Cam arched an eyebrow.

"You work for them?"

Gabe dipped his chin wordlessly. A wave of shyness washed over him at the respect and admiration dawning on the faces of the two men staring at him.

"You're right," Joe said after a moment's hesitation. "They don't normally do clubs."

Gabe blinked at his guarded tone.

Cam eyed Joe shrewdly before clinking his glass against the latter's and raising it in a toast at Gabe.

"Here's to a job well done."

Gabe swallowed and acknowledged the praise with a tilt of his head. He felt Cam's gaze boring into him as he took a sip of his drink. Gabe's chest tightened, heat flooding his body at the feel of those gray eyes caressing his skin.

They made him feel exposed. Vulnerable. As if he were naked, the club empty but for the two of them, the distance between their bodies shrinking with every beat of their hearts.

He gulped down his drink and climbed off the barstool, panic making his body stiff.

"Excuse me."

CHAPTER FOUR

GABE SPLASHED COLD WATER ON HIS FACE BEFORE gripping the edge of the black marble countertop. He stared in the mirror, the tension tightening his skin and threading through his body making it hard to breathe.

He barely recognized the wild-eyed, flushed stranger looking back at him.

I don't think I'm ready for this.

A man came out of one of the stalls. He hesitated when he saw Gabe, but then proceeded to hastily wash his hands and leave the restroom, the door swinging shut behind him.

Gabe dropped his head and closed his eyes. Coming to *Saron* had been a mistake after all. Though he was loathed to admit it, he needed more time before he could follow through with the insane idea he'd come up with tonight.

A sigh left his lips. He'd been in the restroom long enough. It was time to leave while he still had a modicum of pride left. He only hoped there was a back door he could slink out of to avoid the man waiting for him at the bar.

Hinges squeaked behind him. The door opened and closed once more.

Gabe stiffened when he felt a presence at his back. A shiver ran down his spine. He didn't have to open his eyes to know who was standing there. He steeled himself before raising his head and meeting Cam's gaze in the mirror.

Stormy gray locked on blue.

Gabe's mouth went dry at the expression in the gunmetal depths boring into him.

"What are you doing here?" he rasped.

"You were taking too long," Cam replied.

Gabe's pulse jumped. He turned and backed up against the counter as Cam stepped toward him.

Cam stopped a couple of inches away, his commanding presence all the more overwhelming in the confines of the club's restroom.

"What are you running from, Gabe?" he said softly.

Gabe blinked at the blunt question.

"I'm not running from anything," he blurted.

The words rang false even to his ears.

Cam cocked his head slightly to the side and fixed Gabe with a heated stare, curiosity clashing with desire in his molten gaze.

"I'll make this simple. I want you." He raised his right hand and stroked Gabe's lower lip with his thumb, his eyes darkening as they arrowed in on Gabe's mouth. "And I know you want me."

Gabe shivered at Cam's electrifying touch. *SO fucking screwed.* He licked his lips unconsciously.

Cam froze, his pupils dilating as Gabe's tongue darted out and flicked his thumb. His breath stilled for a moment before shuddering out of his chest. He moved, one leg parting Gabe's thighs so he could press his body against his, his hand moving from Gabe's face to the back of his neck to angle his head.

Gabe's eyes widened when Cam swooped in and took his mouth.

They stared at each other for a timeless moment, hot breaths mingling as Cam sensuously molded his lips to Gabe's, learning the contours of each other's mouths. He bit down gently on Gabe's lower lip and tugged.

Holy shit.

Gabe's cock twitched at the erotic move, a low moan vibrating through him.

Cam's fingers tightened in Gabe's hair. He parted Gabe's lips roughly, gray eyes shifting to the color of a stormy sea, his thigh pressing up against Gabe's swelling arousal. His other hand found Gabe's left butt cheek, fingers digging into the taut flesh as he ground their lower bodies together.

Gabe gasped at the rock-hard feel of Cam's erection against his hip. Cam swept past his teeth at his sharp inhale and invaded his mouth, their tongues meeting in a possessive mating dance that made Gabe weak at the knees. Gabe's eyes fluttered closed. His toes curled and his fingers found the edge of the countertop before he lost all strength.

Waves of heat flooded his entire body where Cam touched him. He couldn't think, couldn't breathe, could do nothing except focus his entire being on the man who was masterfully claiming him.

He never knew a kiss could feel this good.

Cam tightened his hold on Gabe, their heated pants merging while he licked and sucked Gabe's tongue before biting down.

Oh, sweet Jesus!

Gabe's hips thrust forward reflexively, his cock pushing against Cam while the latter maintained his devastating assault on his mouth. Blood pounded in his ears, his heartbeat impossibly fast. He felt Cam guide him away from the sink and blinked his eyes open.

Cam backed him across the restroom to a stall at the far end, his lips never leaving Gabe's. Gabe closed his eyes again, a golden haze of pleasure washing across him. The sound of a bolt sliding home reached his ears dimly. Cam pushed him against a tiled wall and reached down. There was the clink of a belt and the slide of a zipper.

Gabe's stomach contracted when Cam's hand brushed his hard-on. Fingers tugged at his briefs. Cool air washed over his naked cock as it sprang free.

Gabe stiffened, a flash of fear darting through him.

Cam's fingers closed around his flesh.

Gabe's eyes slammed open, shocked at the feel of another man's hand on his most intimate part after so long. He met Cam's sultry stare and dragged his mouth from his, breaking the kiss. Their breaths filled the confined space as they lowered their gazes to where Cam palmed Gabe's cock.

Gabe bit back a moan as he watched Cam's fingers move up his shaft, the long, thick thumb gliding across the shiny, veiny surface before sliding across the sensitive pink head, capturing the drops pearling at the tip.

"Beautiful," Cam breathed.

Gabe looked up and almost came at the feverish expression on Cam's face.

Oh God.

All reason and fear fled Gabe as Cam started rubbing him, his touch made slick by Gabe's pre-cum. Cam leaned forward, his head nudging Gabe's chin up, his lips finding his throat. He pressed his other hand against the wall next to Gabe's head, his breaths coming slow and hard through his nose, his arousal a stiff rod poking Gabe's thigh.

Pleasure surged through Gabe as Cam increased the pace of his wrist, his hand occasionally dropping to caress and play with the sac at the base of Gabe's cock before moving to the main event once more. The sweet friction of Cam's fingers on Gabe's rock-hard shaft sent delicious waves of sensation swirling through Gabe's lower body.

Gabe's balls tingled and tightened as the first waves of his climax gathered at the base of his spine and his throbbing cock.

"Oh, fuck." Gabe spread his arms and braced his hands against the walls, fingers clutching desperately at the white tiles while he thrust his hips into Cam's grip.

"That's right." Cam sucked and repeatedly bit the sensitive skin of Gabe's neck before licking and kissing it. His fingers stroked Gabe faster and faster, the wet slide of his palm against Gabe's aching flesh an erotic soundtrack that had pre-cum leaking almost continually from the flushed tip. "Come for me."

Gabe gasped at the explicit command, body tightening like a coiled spring, his cock twitching and straining in Cam's hand. He could almost taste his orgasm, he was so close.

Cam kept up his tormenting pace on Gabe's shaft and reached down with his other hand, finding the stretch of taut skin between the base of Gabe's balls and his ass.

Gabe stiffened at the unfamiliar sensation, not sure if he liked it.

"Cam?"

Cam brought his lips to Gabe's ear.

"Don't think," he whispered, his hot breath sending shivers across Gabe's skin. "Just feel."

His palm moved rapidly up and down Gabe's shaft, sending delicious tension spiraling through Gabe's spine once more. Cam flicked his thumb across the sensitive head at the same time that he pressed his fingers against a tight spot under his balls.

Stars exploded behind Gabe's eyes.

"Oh! Oh, yes!"

Gabe arched, head falling back against the wall as intense pleasure erupted from deep inside his belly and flooded his entire body. Cam's name was a breathless chant on his lips between the passionate moans and grunts being ripped from his throat. Shudders shook him, his climax sending his cock pulsing and throbbing, filling the hand pleasuring him with hot cum.

The orgasm lasted long, earth-shattering seconds, a white haze of ecstasy that filled Gabe's consciousness and sent blinding spots flickering across his inner vision. He rode the exquisite waves until they started to fade, his hips moving in rolling deep thrusts, his ass clenching and unclenching, his legs trembling. The harsh sound of his ragged pants were drowned by the buzz of blood in his ears.

It wasn't until Gabe's heartbeat started to slow and awareness returned that he realized he was gripping Cam's shoulders for support, his forehead resting in the crook of Cam's neck and his breaths washing across the toned, tan skin at the opening of his shirt.

Gentle fingers tilted his chin up. Gabe blinked and met Cam's gaze dazedly, still basking in the afterglow of the most incredible orgasm he had ever had, utterly stunned by what had just transpired.

He had never known such soul shattering pleasure before.

"You are so fucking sexy," Cam whispered, his gunmetal gaze bright with desire. He lowered his mouth to Gabe's, delivering a burning kiss that made his toes curl and sent tingles all over his body once more. "Let's get out of here."

CHAPTER FIVE

GABE STOOD UNDER THE SHOWER FOR LONG MINUTES, hands braced against the tiled walls while the hot spray cascaded over his head and shoulders.

He finally reached down and twisted a lever. The sluice of water abated, silence replacing the noisy splash. Warm drops dripped from his wet hair and rolled down his naked skin. He caught sight of himself in the floor-length mirror as he turned and reached for the bath towel.

Gabe stilled, startled. He barely recognized himself.

His cheeks were flushed, his lips swollen from Cam's kisses, his eyes dark with desire and tension. Gabe shivered and dragged his gaze from the sultry stranger in the reflection. He glanced around the steamy, luxurious bathroom once more, not quite believing he'd come here with Cam.

They'd left *Saron* forty minutes ago, escaping the club under Ethan's watchful gaze. Gabe had flashed an apologetic smile at the bartender as Cam led him toward the exit. Ethan had dipped his chin in silent acknowledgment, his expression still wary.

Gabe had blinked when they'd walked out of the alley and emerged onto the noisy Shinjuku strip, the night air cooling his hot cheeks. Cam's fingers had remained firmly clasped around his since the moment they'd left the club restroom, making Gabe wonder whether he'd sensed his sudden nervousness and his renewed urge to bolt.

Getting a hand job from Cam was one thing. Going to bed with the man who had just given him the most perfect orgasm he had ever experienced in his entire life was a completely different ballgame.

Cam had hailed a cab, guided Gabe onto the backseat, and climbed in before he could succumb to the small voice telling him to run. Cam had given the driver an address in flawless Japanese before turning to Gabe.

Gabe had hesitated and was about to speak when Cam scooted across the space separating them and took his lips, his gray eyes blazing with heat and his arousal digging into the side of Gabe's thigh.

Gabe had gasped, stunned by the bold move. He'd glanced sideways and caught the driver's shocked stare in the rearview mirror. A thrill of excitement had run through Gabe when he imagined the sexy, filthy picture he and Cam no doubt made as they kissed in the backseat.

Gabe had opened his mouth and welcomed the man wanting in, his tongue rising to meet the one invading his body. Heat pulsed through him as he closed his eyes and surrendered to pleasure, all thoughts of their avid onlooker fleeing his mind. Cam had groaned at his blatant surrender, his hot pants mingling with Gabe's while he raised his hands and clasped the sides of his head, his fingers twisting in Gabe's hair and angling his head to better plunder his mouth.

By the time the cab had pulled to a stop outside the brightly-lit hotel on the hill overlooking the city, Gabe could barely recall his own name.

Cam Sorvino was a world-class tease and had applied himself most splendidly during their ten-minute ride, fingers touching Gabe everywhere except where he most wanted to be touched, his lips and tongue ravaging Gabe's and bringing on a rock-hard erection.

Gabe had sobered slightly after they'd entered the hotel foyer. He'd waited by a marble pillar while Cam walked over to reception and booked a room, his gaze fixed on the opulent decor as he carefully avoided eye contact with the man behind the desk, hoping he wouldn't be recognized.

His concerns had been blown out of the water in the elevator ride to the twelfth floor. Cam had pressed him against the mirrored wall, his powerful leg nestled between his thighs, his tongue fucking his mouth while he rolled his hips against Gabe's arousal. By the time they'd entered the suite, Gabe had been so hard he knew all it would take was a simple flick of Cam's fingers on his engorged flesh for him to come.

Cam had poured him a drink from the minibar

before heading for the shower, a wickedly filthy smile curving his lips as his gaze dropped to Gabe's erection.

"Don't start without me," he ordered thickly.

Gabe nodded wordlessly, the first tendril of anxiety penetrating his dazed brain.

Cam's gray eyes narrowed as he paused in the doorway to the bathroom. "And don't you dare run."

Gabe stiffened at his warning. He raised his chin challengingly. "I won't."

Cam dipped his head and grinned. "I'll hold you to that."

Gabe took his scotch to the glass wall spanning the width of the suite and stared out into the night while he drank the amber liquid. Even at this hour, lights sparkled all over Tokyo, painting the city in a dazzling colorful display that would only fade with the arrival of dawn.

He pressed a hand to the glass and dropped his head against the cool surface, willing away the fear licking at his feet. The faint sound of the shower and the king-size bed dominating the room served as stark reminders of what was to come.

You can do this.

Gabe had always known this would be the most difficult step. His therapist's warning from his last counseling session rang in his ears once more.

"You will never be able to sleep with another man if you can't get past your trust issues, Gabe. I know this sounds awful, but you will have to put yourself in a vulnerable position again when that time comes. You will be naked, powerless, and totally helpless in the hands of your lover.

And you will have to trust him. Trust that he won't hurt you."

Gabe gritted his teeth and fought to control the panic threatening to overwhelm him.

Though he was surprised at how easy it had been to let Cam touch him, sex was an entirely different matter.

The bathroom door opened behind him. Gabe's mouth went dry as he watched Cam walk out in a billow of steam in the reflection in the glass. He swallowed and turned slowly.

Cam's body was all corded muscles and sinews, his tan skin toned to perfection. A trail of dark hair tapered from his chest and arrowed down his six-pack and navel before disappearing beneath the white towel hanging precariously around his hips and powerful thighs. His hair was slick with moisture and his gray gaze hooded as it landed on Gabe.

Cam crossed the floor, his steps silent on the carpet, and took the glass from Gabe's suddenly weak hand. He swallowed a mouthful of scotch before brushing his lips across Gabe's.

"Your turn," Cam whispered in Gabe's ear.

His low chuckle followed Gabe as he practically bolted for the bathroom.

Sexy bastard.

CHAPTER SIX

Cam's pulse jumped at the sound of the shower being turned off. He leaned back against the leather headboard and crossed his legs, wincing slightly when his cock strained against the thick fabric of the towel. Even though he'd jacked off in the bathroom, he was rock-hard again.

Cam had been shocked by the haunted expression that had flashed across Gabe's face before he'd disappeared in the direction of *Saron*'s restroom earlier that evening after Joe joined them at the bar. Unease had slowly filled him as the minutes ticked by and Gabe still didn't return.

The realization that Gabe was about to run had struck him like a bolt from out of the blue.

Cam had left Joe mid-conversation and tossed a hurried apology at his best friend as he headed for the back of the club, his body moving of its own volition. He couldn't explain the burning desire growing inside him for a man he had just met. There was only one thing Cam was certain of.

He wasn't ready to let go of Gabe Anderson yet.

The relief that shuddered through Cam when he found Gabe in the restroom had startled him. What happened afterward had shaken him to the core.

Cam stilled as he ran his fingers through his damp hair. He stared at his hand and let out a shaky chuckle when he detected the fine tremor running through it. He had not been this horny since his teens. And there was only one person he could blame for his superbly inflamed state.

Gabe was unlike any of his previous conquests. Cam had known this from the moment they touched. Known that this was more than lust. He had never felt this electrifying connection with any man or woman before. Had never experienced this desperate need to get under another person's skin. To feel his heart beat frantically against his own. To watch him shatter beneath him.

This should have been warning enough for the commitment-phobic asshole that he was. There was only one reason he was here, in this hotel room, right now.

Cam had never seen anything as staggeringly beautiful as the sight of Gabe climaxing in his arms. From the sensuous dance of Gabe's hips as he rode his pleasure to the flush of color darkening his chiseled cheekbones. From the glazed look of ecstasy turning his eyes to cobalt to the throaty moans and grunts parting his lips.

Gabe was the definition of every sexy, filthy fantasy Cam had ever had, wrapped in a drop-dead gorgeous package that promised mind-blowing sex.

And Cam wanted it. Wanted it so bad, he could taste it.

He had only one aim in mind for the rest of this night – to fuck Gabe's brains out and watch him orgasm over and over again.

The bathroom door opened. Gabe came out, a towel wrapped around his waist and his expression guarded. He froze when he saw the box of condoms and bottle of lube on the nightstand.

"Where the hell did you get those?"

Cam smiled and folded his arms behind his head.

"I bribed the guy behind the desk when I checked in. It's amazing what some of these places have in their back rooms."

Gabe groaned, a mortified look dawning on his handsome face. He walked over to the bed, sat on the edge, and dropped his head in his hands. Another groan left his lips.

"What?" Cam said, puzzled.

Gabe turned and looked at him, the towel riding tantalizingly high on his thighs.

"You know I work for Damon & Tucker?"

Cam blinked. "Yeah?"

Gabe glanced pointedly around the suite.

"There was a project they put me in charge of since before I got here. A contract that was going to be incredibly lucrative for the firm. The first of a chain of new luxury hotels."

Surprise flashed through Cam.

"You mean — you *designed* this place?"

The hotel's grand opening had been splashed across every paper and newsfeed in the city early that week. Cam had heard nothing but rave reviews about the place since, which was why he'd chosen it for tonight.

Gabe nodded, a crooked smile playing on his lips.

"Yeah. It wasn't just me though. I couldn't have done it without my team."

Cam studied the room with fresh eyes and took in its elegant details, searching for signs of Gabe's touch. Now that he knew what to look for, he could see them everywhere. Like the man sitting on the bed watching him, the suite oozed style and sophistication.

Cam stared at the standing mirror facing the right side of the king-size bed. "Even that?"

Gabe followed his gaze and flushed. "Well, that wasn't strictly my idea."

Cam looked up and grinned. "We could have done with one on the ceiling."

Gabe scowled. "This is not a sex hotel. And I know it's a bit late to say this now, but I'm beginning to suspect that you're a pervert."

Cam chuckled. "I'm not going to deny it."

Gabe threw his head back and laughed. The sound danced along Cam's spine and made the hairs rise on his skin.

"Come here," Cam said huskily. He held out a hand.

Gabe hesitated. He climbed on the bed and slowly scooted over.

Cam flashed his teeth before grabbing Gabe's arm and jerking him close.

Gabe swore when he landed hard against Cam's chest.

"Up you go," Cam drawled.

He heaved Gabe until he had him sitting on his lap with his knees denting the mattress on either side of Cam's thighs. Cam wrapped his arms around Gabe's back and pulled him in. A shudder ran through them both when their naked chests made contact, the feeling as electrifying as their first kiss.

"That's better," Cam growled.

He reached up and flicked his tongue against Gabe's chin before tugging his head down and taking his mouth.

Gabe's eyes darkened above him, his hips flexing in response to the passionate kiss while his tongue clashed with Cam's. Cam swallowed a curse when Gabe's towel-covered cock rocked against his stomach. He thrust up, his dick twitching against the inside of Gabe's left thigh.

※

"Oh!"

Gabe wrenched his mouth free and gasped when Cam's erection pushed up between his legs and grazed his thigh. Cam ran his hands down Gabe's arms, his fingers stroking and squeezing the taut muscles before moving to Gabe's chest.

Gabe sucked air between his teeth when Cam

brushed the pads of his thumbs across his nipples, stunned at the jolt of electricity that arrowed down from them to his groin. Seeing his reaction, Cam repeated the movement.

"Fuck!" Gabe's eyes widened when the shocking sensation recurred.

Cam moved his mouth along Gabe's jawline to his left ear while he continued playing with his chest. He worked the lobe, nibbling and licking it with his clever teeth and lips, his heated breath sending shivers racing down Gabe's spine while he pinched and pulled at his nipples.

A low cry of need escaped Gabe as pleasure rippled through his body. He arched, his head dropping back, his hands rising to grip the leather headboard behind Cam, his hips thrusting helplessly against the man cradling him, his pre-cum staining the towel.

"Jesus, Gabe," Cam rasped, his own hips rolling beneath Gabe.

Cam's towel had fallen open and his hot, naked cock brushed and nudged the inside of Gabe's left thigh. His mouth moved south, kissing and nipping Gabe's throat before laving the sting with his tongue.

Gabe's heart stuttered when Cam shifted his lips to his left nipple, his fingers still pinching and pulling at his right one. He trembled as Cam licked the hard nub before flicking it with his tongue and running tight circles around it for several mind-blowing seconds.

Gabe looked down and met Cam's heated stare a second before he opened his mouth and took his aroused flesh inside.

"Oh God, *Cam!*"

Gabe's fingers bit into the headboard as Cam sucked one nipple and then the other, each powerful contraction of his lips and mouth sending a numbing bolt of pleasure to Gabe's cock. Shocked flared through Gabe as he felt an orgasm gather at the base of his balls.

"No *fucking* way," Gabe moaned brokenly, his startled gaze clashing with the blazing gunmetal stare beneath him.

Cam sucked harder, hands reaching under the towel to palm Gabe's clenched butt cheeks. He squeezed and massaged the tense muscles before moving down his thighs and around to the front.

Gabe stiffened when Cam's fingers touched his hard shaft. He ran them lightly up the sides, his nails grazing the twitching, engorged flesh. He paused just before he reached the sensitive head, his touch a hairbreadth away, his eyes darting up to meet Gabe's.

Gabe swallowed when he registered the silent command in the gray depths.

"Cam." Heat flooded Gabe's cheeks at the sound of his need-filled voice. "*Please.*"

Cam acknowledged his tortured plea with a groan. He tugged on Gabe's left nipple with his teeth at the same time as he stroked the pad of one thumb across the tip of his shaft.

Gabe's breath locked in his throat as his climax hit him hard. He convulsed against Cam, his cock twitching and pulsing, his cum soaking the towel.

CHAPTER SEVEN

CAM GRITTED HIS TEETH, THE TORTURED SOUNDS coming from Gabe's lips inflaming his senses as he came apart in his arms. Cam yanked away the towels covering their bodies, lifted Gabe, and twisted him around before pushing him down on the bed. A shudder ran through him when he covered the body of the beautiful man still climaxing from his touch with his own. He took Gabe's mouth roughly and swallowed his grunts while the latter's hips jerked beneath him in the final throes of his orgasm.

Cam reached out blindly, grabbed the bottle of lube from the nightstand, and wrenched his lips from Gabe's. He sat back on his heels and poured a generous amount of the liquid in his right hand before dropping the bottle on the bed. He hooked his left hand behind Gabe's right knee, bent his leg, and pushed his thigh to the side, opening him up for his touch. Gabe blinked dazedly as Cam reached down, lubed fingers skimming past his trembling balls and the stretch of taut skin behind it.

&a,

GABE FROZE WHEN HE FELT CAM'S WET FINGER SLIDE against the tight pucker of his ass. A half-choked whimper escaped his throat despite his best effort to stifle it. The sweet post-orgasmic afterglow bathing his body evaporated in a chill of pure terror.

All of a sudden, Gabe was there again. In that filthy, run-down hotel room the night when his life changed forever. That terrible, awful night when five men had held him down on a dirty bed sticky with their own cum. Five men who had watched him with crazy eyes while they tore the clothes off his body, their faces filled with lust. Five men who had raked his skin and flesh with their hands, teeth, and tongues and jerked off over him while he fought them desperately, his body weak and his mind fuzzy from the drug they'd slipped him.

No, that that *bastard* had slipped him.

The man Gabe had mistakenly fallen in love with. The first person he'd ever wanted to give himself to. The one who had sat in a chair opposite the bed, watching him with an excited gleam in his eyes, one hand frantically working his erection while he held a camera in the other. He'd continued filming while Gabe shouted as his legs were violently pulled apart, his entire body stiffening in horror when a stranger pressed his bare cock against his hole, the first of the five men who had paid to rape him on tape.

Cam stilled above him, bringing him back to the present. His face sobered and his hands paused on Gabe's body.

"Hey," he said softly, concern flashing in his eyes, "are you okay?"

Gabe bit his lip and shook his head. He sat up and scooted away until his back met the headboard, one hand rising to clutch at his hair, remorse and self-hatred filling him.

"I'm—I'm sorry. I don't think I can do this," he whispered.

Cam frowned. Gabe's stomach twisted as he watched his puzzled expression turn to disbelief.

"Is this your first time?" Cam said, shocked.

Gabe tried to push down the pain that rose inside him when Cam physically pulled back from him. Even though he had wanted Cam to stop, he could not help the acute sense of loss that tore through him at his shocked expression and strained posture.

"Technically, yes," Gabe said with a low, derisive chuckle.

Cam knelt on the bed, his gloriously swollen dick visibly shrinking as he watched Gabe.

"What do you mean, technically?"

Gabe inhaled shakily, his hands fisting while he fought the sudden wave of nausea roiling through his belly. This was it. The moment he had been dreading all along. Ever since he accepted Cam's invitation at the bar. No, ever since he decided to move to Tokyo and start over again.

Gabe knew that if he wanted to overcome the emotional and physical wounds of his past, to have a chance at any kind of meaningful relationship in the future, to finally heal the scars embedded in his soul, then he had to brave this man's reaction to learning why he couldn't handle having sex, right here and now. He took a shuddering breath.

"If you discount the five guys who tried to rape me while my supposed boyfriend watched on with a camera in hand, then, yes, this is technically my first time."

Gabe heard Cam's sharp intake of breath and dared himself to look at the face of the first man he had wanted to sleep with in nearly a decade.

The expression in Cam's eyes nearly undid him. Instead of disgust, all Gabe read in the stormy gaze was anger and compassion.

"Tell me," Cam said between gritted teeth. He turned to sit on the edge of the bed.

Gabe wrapped his arms around his raised knees. "Not much to tell really. It was eight years ago. I was in my final year of design school and my first ever relationship with a man." He swallowed. "I always suspected I was gay. Although I'd dated girls in high school and college, I wasn't sure until the day I met him."

"What was that asshole's name?" Cam growled.

"Andrew," Gabe breathed. The old hurt twisted through his heart once more at the sound of his former lover's name. It had been years since he last said it out loud. More than four years. In fact, the last time was during his final session with his therapist in Chicago. "His name is Andrew."

"What did he do?"

Gabe blinked at the rage in Cam's voice. The fact that this sexy, gorgeous man, this king, had not rejected him and appeared instead to be utterly livid at what had happened to him was enough to give Gabe the courage he'd desperately been seeking. The words came tumbling out of his mouth, confessions he had only ever revealed to the therapist he had been referred to by the detectives in charge of his case. He shared how he had fallen wildly and madly in love with the first man who had ever properly given him any attention and made him feel wanted. It was a relationship he had fully trusted in.

It was only afterward that Gabe realized Andrew had always backed out whenever he wanted to have penetrative sex. They had kissed and fooled around plenty of times and given each other hundreds of hand jobs. They had even sucked each other's dicks, although Gabe had gone down on Andrew ten times more than he ever did him. Andrew's excuse had always been the same: the timing wasn't right. That he wasn't ready yet, even though Gabe had made it clear that he would be the receiving partner in their relationship.

In his filthiest dreams, Gabe had only ever had one wish. To be taken. To be made love to by a man. To be fucked and driven wild with pleasure while someone rammed his dick into his body, branding his insides, possessing him, controlling him.

It wasn't until the night of their first anniversary together, the night he'd thought Andrew would finally fulfill his dirtiest wishes, the night he had waited so long for — to finally welcome another man inside the place no one had touched before — that the truth had finally come out.

CHAPTER EIGHT

"IT SEEMED HE WAS PART OF THIS—" GABE NEARLY SPAT
out the words, his bitterness threatening to boil over,
"—this group of sick men who enjoyed raping gay
guys on camera. They were mostly straight. Or
pretending to be anyway. There'd been a few cases
reported in the local news that year. Of gay men
being found in dark alleys, some nearly dead, all
violently beaten and gang-raped. All drugged. All
tricked and trapped by someone they'd thought
cared for them." Gabe stared at the white sheets
where he'd been lying with Cam moments ago, rage
and shame burning through him. "I'd never paid
attention to those stories." A tortured chuckle
escaped his throat. "I mean, why would I, right? After
all, I was in a relationship. I had someone who I
thought loved me. Someone I was willing to give
myself to—"

"Stop it," Cam said in a hard voice.

Gabe looked up and found Cam's steady gaze on

him. A myriad of emotions welled up inside Gabe at the tenderness in Cam's eyes.

"Stop blaming yourself for something that was not your fault," Cam said quietly. "That bastard is an asshole and what he did to you was unforgivable." He scowled. "I hope they got what they deserved, he and those fuckers who raped you."

"They did." Gabe smiled tremulously. "And they didn't."

Cam stared at him, puzzled.

"Someone in the next room heard the commotion," Gabe said. "I put up quite a fight despite the drug Andrew slipped me. The hotel manager came knocking at the door after I kicked over the nightstand."

Cam's pupils flared. "You mean—"

Gabe dipped his chin.

"They didn't rape me." A shiver ran down Gabe's spine at his own murmured confession. That had been his only salvation from that entire despicable night. The fact that those men hadn't managed to do what they'd so clearly intended to. "They couldn't. They hadn't prepped me. I was too tight." Heat flooded his cheeks. "Andrew had never even fingered me."

Cam raised an eyebrow, his gaze roaming Gabe from his head all the way to his toes, as if he couldn't quite believe what he was hearing. Fire danced along Gabe's skin where the gray eyes landed.

"And you never — you know, did it yourself before?" Cam said.

Gabe burrowed his face in his hands, suddenly embarrassed.

"I had," he mumbled. "But I was terrified to do it after what happened. My therapist recommended I keep trying. He said it was the only way I would get over the fear of being penetrated. He even recommended I use sex toys."

Cam stirred on the bed. "And did you?"

Gabe blinked at Cam's tone. He looked up and saw avid curiosity mixed with concern on Cam's face.

Gabe smiled drily. "The first time I tried a butt plug, I nearly passed out."

Cam looked down at his dick. Gabe flushed when he realized Cam was getting aroused again. Surprisingly, he felt a stirring in his own groin.

"This is bigger than a butt plug," Cam said, deadpan.

Laughter bubbled inside Gabe, catching him off guard.

"It sure is."

Cam's expression grew serious. He watched Gabe for silent seconds.

"What happened at the club between us…was it good? As good as any of the stuff…" A muscle jumped in Cam's cheek. "…*he* ever did to you?"

Gabe's breath caught in his throat at the question.

"No."

Cam's expression fell so comically Gabe almost laughed again.

"It was a hundred times better," Gabe admitted huskily, cheeks warming as his confession rang in his ears.

Relief and desire flashed in Cam's eyes. He hesitated for a moment while he considered Gabe.

"One night. Give me one night to show you how good it can be."

Gabe stared. A chuckle left his lips. "God, I can't believe you said something that corny with a straight face."

The corner of Cam's mouth lifted in a stunningly sexy smile. He raised an eyebrow. "You ain't seen nothing yet." Cam sobered. "I mean it, Gabe. One night."

The air thickened between them, filling with sexual tension and that electrifying aura that seemed to surround them whenever they were close to one another, making it hard to breathe.

Cam sat quietly two feet from him. Watching. Waiting. As if he had all the time in the world.

Gabe hesitated. He could feel himself standing on the edge of a precipice, one he had willingly come to. If he said no, he would walk out of this room a scarred man, unable to let himself be touched by another man. If he said yes, he would be entering unknown territory with someone who was still a perfect stranger to him. One who had the potential to hurt him as much as pleasure him.

Cam's next words sealed his fate.

"You can trust me, Gabe. I would never do anything to hurt you."

Gabe closed his eyes briefly, unable to meet the devastatingly beautiful gray stare opposite him. He took a shallow breath and stepped off the cliff.

"Okay."

CAM MOVED, THE MATTRESS SHIFTING UNDER HIM, HIS pulse racing wildly. Never in a million years could he have guessed the dark secrets Gabe had been keeping inside his heart. Cam could see how much it had cost him to confess the terrible things that had happened to him at the hands of his former lover.

Deep beneath the desire Cam harbored for Gabe, the anger he felt toward the monsters who had hurt him still simmered in his veins. That they had dared to try and destroy this beautiful man was something Cam could never forgive.

That was when he realized something else besides passion and outrage was twisting his gut. Cam blinked as he finally recognized a jealous, possessive streak he never even knew he possessed.

He pushed this startling discovery aside and considered the achingly gorgeous man before him.

"Do you want me?"

Gabe swallowed before dipping his chin. His eyes flared when he glanced down and saw Cam's growing arousal.

"Good. Because I'm going to give you the best night of your life. By the time I'm finished with you, your ass is going to be aching for my dick."

Gabe shivered at his words, a flush of color darkening his cheekbones.

Cam leaned forward and placed his hands on Gabe's knees, gently parting them. Gabe watched him cautiously as he settled between his thighs.

"First," Cam raised his left hand to caress Gabe's face before rubbing his thumb across his lips, "I'm going to kiss that delicious body of yours. All. Over."

Gabe twitched. He opened his mouth, his breath accelerating. His tongue darted out. Cam shuddered when Gabe licked his thumb, the pink flesh wet and hot against his skin. He trailed the fingers of his right hand down Gabe's chest, his own breathing speeding up as excitement filled him.

"Then, I'm going to give you the best blow job you've ever had."

Gabe moaned when Cam pushed his thumb inside his mouth and past his teeth. He closed his lips and tongue around it and started to suck, his ice-blue eyes darkening with anticipation.

Cam swallowed a curse at the sensual sight, his shaft twitching at the arousing sensation of Gabe's strong jaw and mouth working his finger. He brushed his hand across the taut muscles below Gabe's navel and smiled when they trembled and jerked beneath his touch.

Cam leaned forward and brought his mouth to Gabe's right ear.

"After that, I'm going to get your hole so ready for me, you'll be melting with pleasure," he murmured.

Gabe groaned, his head falling back, causing Cam's thumb to pop out of his mouth with a wet sound as his hips flexed off the mattress, his hands fisting in the bedsheets on either side of him.

Cam dipped his head and kissed Gabe's throat, his lips finding the strong pulse hammering away wildly a couple of inches above his left collarbone. He licked and sucked that spot for several seconds before coming up and bringing his mouth a hair's breadth from Gabe's.

Cam stared into the glazed blue depths opposite him and gave Gabe a full-blown teasing grin.

"Then, I'll wait. Until you're begging for it."

CHAPTER NINE

OH, SWEET JESUS!

Sanity fled Gabe at Cam's sexy, filthy words, all thoughts of his past, work, and the hotel room where he was escaping his mind as he moaned and grabbed Cam's face. He closed the gap between them, his lips rough as he kissed the man mercilessly taunting him.

Cam opened his mouth and welcomed him inside, his tongue wrapping around Gabe's in a move that had him rolling his hips off the mattress again. Gabe groaned, his ass twitching from the torrid images Cam had painted for him, anticipation buzzing through his veins at the thought of all the exquisitely wicked things that were about to happen to his body.

Cam clasped Gabe's nape and tugged on the back of his left thigh. He guided Gabe slowly down onto his back before carefully settling his powerful frame in the cradle of Gabe's thighs.

Emotion choked Gabe at the tender way Cam was treating him despite the passion burning through them both. He wrenched his mouth from their kiss and locked his arms around Cam's wide shoulders before burying his face in the crook of Cam's neck. A single tear spilled from his eye.

He had never known such gentleness.

Cam froze.

"Do you want me to—"

"No!" Gabe dug his fingers in Cam's skin and gripped Cam's hips with his thighs as the latter started to pull away. "Don't," he breathed. "Don't stop."

Cam propped himself up on one elbow and looked down at him. His pupils flared and darkened. He raised a finger and wiped the wetness at the corner of Gabe's right eye.

"I won't," he whispered.

His mouth met Gabe's in a soft kiss before he moved his lips to Gabe's left ear.

Gabe shivered as Cam kissed, licked, and sucked the lobe before moving to the other side. Like he'd promised he would, Cam worked his way down Gabe's body, his hands, mouth, and tongue branding a blistering path along Gabe's skin that had him writhing and arching off the bed.

He never knew his body had so many erogenous areas until Cam uncovered them one by one, his pace unhurried while he drove Gabe completely and utterly wild. Having touched and kissed him everywhere on his front except for his dick and balls, Cam turned Gabe onto his belly and started on his back. Gabe buried his face in the pillow and fisted his hands in the sheets, unable to control his thrusting hips and throaty moans as Cam's tongue and lips danced down his spine and roamed his flesh. His balls tightened, the sweet tension heralding his impending orgasm.

Gabe came when Cam found the spot behind his left knee, hoarse cries leaving his lips while he pumped his pulsing cock into the mattress.

"Cam! *Oh God!*"

Cam continued kissing him, his tongue laving the sensitive area while Gabe's climax washed over him, his heated pants warming Gabe's skin.

Gabe collapsed on the bed when the final twitches faded, his mind a hazy, gooey mush, his heart thundering against his ribs, his ragged breathing loud in his ears.

"Was that good?" Cam said huskily, dropping a searing kiss on his back.

Gabe could only nod, too dazed to speak.

"Great," Cam purred. "We're just getting started."

Cam rolled Gabe onto his back, bent his knees, and pressed strong hands against the inside of his thighs. He pushed Gabe's legs apart, exposing him to his gaze.

Gabe barely had time to register his intent before Cam moved down and brought his mouth to Gabe's dick.

Holy shit!

Gabe sucked air between his teeth as Cam's tongue flicked the slit of his still-leaking cock. Then, the full lips that had just brought him to his third earth-shattering orgasm of the night closed around the tip of Gabe's shaft and sucked gently while his wicked tongue whirled across the sensitive flesh.

"Cam!"

Cam closed his fingers around Gabe's throbbing length and played him while his mouth swallowed him farther inside. Gabe gasped, pleasure flashing red across his brain, his hands finding the back of Cam's head. He couldn't believe he was hard again.

All his senses focused on the fingers, lips, and tongue working his dick and balls. Licking him, nibbling him, oh so skillfully sucking him and drawing out his pre-cum over and over again while his cock twitched helplessly.

Gabe twisted his fingers in Cam's hair when tightness knotted his stomach and thighs. He dug his heels into the bed and flexed his hips.

Cam grunted as the motion sent Gabe's cock deep into his mouth. He took him in greedily, his hands moving down to cup Gabe's butt cheeks, supporting him as he continued to thrust upward. The wet sounds Cam's lips made as they moved up and down Gabe's shaft were so erotic he knew he would never forget them for as long as he lived.

Gabe's eyes widened dazedly when he felt the first waves of his climax coil in the base of his spine. He tugged at Cam's head.

"Cam, I'm gonna—"

Cam resisted Gabe's attempt to pull him off his cock and took his shaft all the way to the back of his throat. He sucked him powerfully before swirling his tongue across the sensitive head.

"Fuck!"

Gabe closed his eyes and cried out, waves of

pleasure rocking him as his cock pulsed and throbbed inside Cam's mouth. Cam swallowed and continued sucking and milking him while he came, prolonging his orgasm for torturous moments.

By the time Gabe collapsed on the bed, sweat had soaked his skin and the muscles of his belly trembled and ached from his long, deep climax. He didn't think he could take much more of the devastating havoc Cam was wreaking on his body.

"Jesus, you're so sexy, Gabe," Cam said huskily.

Gabe's eyes fluttered open.

Cam knelt between his thighs, his hand slowly working his own rock-hard cock, his face flushed with desire.

Heat flashed through Gabe. He rose to his knees and clasped Cam's face, tugging his head down.

"Hey, I just—" Cam protested.

"Shut up, you cocktease," Gabe muttered.

He swallowed Cam's chuckle with his lips and probed his mouth, the taste and scent of his own cum on another man's tongue sending a shiver of need down his spine. Gabe dropped one hand to Cam's dick.

"Let me," he whispered against Cam's lips.

Cam's pupils darkened, his breaths coming hard and fast. He nodded and let go of his shaft as he sat back on his heels, his face and body glistening with a fine sheen of sweat.

Gabe slowly explored Cam's hot cock, his heart hammering away as he caressed the glistening, veiny surface and flushed tip, wondering how it would feel inside of him. His ass contracted at that filthy thought.

Cam clenched his teeth and groaned. His head fell back and he flexed his powerful hips, thrusting his dick through Gabe's fingers. Gabe started stroking Cam, matching the rhythm of his thrusts. A shudder coursed through him as he watched Cam take pleasure from his touch.

Shit, he's the sexy one.

Gabe leaned down and did what he'd been dying to do since he saw Cam's naked body.

Cam froze when Gabe took him inside his mouth.

"Gabe? You don't—"

Gabe wrapped his lips and tongue around the twitching shaft and sucked once.

"Oh Christ," Cam growled. He leaned back and grabbed the bedsheets in a white-knuckled grip.

Gabe moaned and worked him with his mouth and fingers, recalling the way Cam had skillfully sucked him minutes ago. His gaze sought and found the mirror next to the bed. The sight that met his eyes made his cock ache. Him on his knees, his blue eyes dark with desire and his flushed cheeks bulging as he took another man inside his mouth.

Above him, Cam strained, his entire body rigid with tension while he rolled his hips, fucking Gabe's mouth with his dick, beads of sweat pearling his forehead and upper lip.

Gabe shuddered when Cam's gaze met his in the mirror. Cam's eyes were a window to his lust, the sight of their sexy, filthy reflection evidently arousing him as much as it did Gabe. He bit his lower lip and twisted a hand through Gabe's hair, guiding him to suck his shaft just the way he liked it, harsh grunts of pleasure leaving his throat.

Gabe groaned, his tongue and lips moving in a cadence that matched Cam's thrusts. He accelerated the pace and took Cam to the back of his throat.

Cam stiffened, a guttural sound on his lips. His hips rolled deeper, his rhythm growing erratic as he neared his orgasm.

Gabe reached down and scraped his nails lightly over the tightening sac beneath Cam's dick.

"Yes! Oh, fuck!"

Cam exploded inside Gabe's mouth, his cock throbbing and pulsing as he came, filling Gabe's throat repeatedly with his hot cum. Gabe gulped it greedily, lips and tongue working the jerking shaft, drawing out Cam's climax for as long as he could.

CHAPTER TEN

Cam shuddered, waves of ecstasy washing through his body and filling his mind, his entire being tingling from the mind-blowing orgasm Gabe had just given him. He looked down when Gabe finally let go of his dick, his shaft popping out of Gabe's mouth with a wet sound that made his belly clench painfully.

Gabe wiped his mouth and grinned, his face flushed.

"Looks like you enjoyed that."

"We're not done yet," Cam growled. "Get ready for phase three."

Gabe gasped when Cam pushed him down on the bed and settled between his thighs, his blue eyes darkening in anticipation. Cam clasped Gabe's head and kissed him deep and hard. Another groan left his lips when he tasted himself on Gabe's tongue.

Gabe moaned into his mouth, his cock stirring and brushing against Cam's stomach where they lay skin to bare skin.

Cam wrenched his lips free and nudged Gabe's chin up, his lips moving to his throat. He made his way down Gabe's body once more, his mouth leaving a sensuous wet trail that had the man below him cursing and arching into him.

Cam reached for one of the pillows and slipped it under Gabe's ass, lifting his hips. Gabe stilled, muscles tensing as he looked down to where Cam knelt between his legs.

Cam dropped a kiss on the inside of Gabe's right thigh before licking and sucking his stiff flesh.

"Relax, Gabe," he murmured against his skin.

Gabe hesitated before nodding wordlessly, his body slowly unknotting.

Cam reached for the bottle of lube, poured out a generous amount, and warmed the liquid between his hands under Gabe's intense stare. He grinned and palmed Gabe's cock.

"*Shit!*" Gabe startled, the expression flashing across his face telling Cam that wasn't what he'd expected.

Cam started rubbing Gabe's shaft with his slick fingers and swallowed a groan as he watched Gabe's confusion turn to pleasure. He leaned down, laved the sensitive head of Gabe's cock with his tongue, and was rewarded with another colorful curse.

Cam played with Gabe's dick and balls until he was thrashing and moaning below him before sliding his thumb down to the taut stretch of skin behind his sac. He rubbed it and pressed.

"*Oh God!*"

Gabe's cock jerked in Cam's grip. His thighs parted

and his knees dropped open as he bucked and lifted his ass off the pillow.

It was all the invitation Cam had been waiting for. He pressed his hands against the back of Gabe's thighs and pushed them while he leaned down. A hungry grunt left him as his eyes finally found the hidden pucker of skin he'd been dying to see since he first laid eyes on Gabe.

It was as sexy as the rest of him.

He flicked it with his tongue.

HOLY. FUCK.

Gabe's breath hitched in his throat at the feel of Cam's tongue against his hole. His whole body tightened and tingled at the alien sensation. He was wondering whether he liked it or not when Cam repeated the move. Brightness flashed across Gabe's vision. A guttural moan of need ripped out of his throat, catching him by surprise.

Like it. Definitely like it!

Cam licked and kissed his hole over and over again until he was thoroughly wet and trembling like crazy. Only then did he bring his slick thumb into play.

Gabe shivered as Cam circled his hole with a feather light touch, the move matching his stiff tongue as he alternated with flicking and teasing his folds. A delicious ache built deep inside Gabe's ass at the devastating assault. Cam pressed another finger against the taut skin below Gabe's balls, digging into the same spot that had made him see stars the first time he touched it.

"*Oh!*"

Gabe bit his lip as his hole clenched tightly, pleasure shooting through his entire body.

"That's it, Gabe," Cam said huskily. "Tighten, just like that. It'll make it easier."

Gabe nodded shakily. He obeyed Cam's murmured commands despite his confusion, squeezing tighter and tighter. His eyes widened when he felt his hole start to relax and give way.

That was when Cam pressed his thumb against Gabe's quivering opening and slid inside.

"Cam!" Gabe gasped, shocked at how easy and painless it was compared to when he'd fingered himself.

Cam gently bit the inside of Gabe's thigh, causing him to hiss in pleasure. He moved up and started to play with Gabe's cock again, licking and sucking the quivering shaft, his thumb still wedged inside Gabe's twitching hole.

Tension wound through Gabe. He tightened again, squeezing Cam, his cheeks warming when he realized he'd sucked him in further.

"That's it," Cam purred around his cock. "God, your ass feels so great, Gabe. I can't wait to get inside you."

Gabe moaned, his past fears evaporating at the blistering image that flashed across his inner vision. Of Cam taking him, his cock sliding in and out of his body, his hips pumping hard against Gabe's ass while he drove them both wild with the fast, intense friction. Seconds later, his hole started to relax again.

Cam grabbed the bottle of lube and poured it directly where his thumb met Gabe's body. Gabe shivered at the cool sensation. He forgot all about it in the next instant.

Cam had withdrawn his thumb and was sliding it back inside.

Gabe's body lifted off the bed, a hoarse cry on his lips as Cam continued thrusting his thumb in and out of his hungry, aching hole.

"Again, Gabe. Tighten again!" Cam ordered between gritted teeth.

Gabe's head thrashed on the pillow as he obeyed, fiery pleasure burning through him from where Cam fucked him with his thumb.

His eyes widened when Cam suddenly withdrew, poured more lube on his hand, and brought two fingers to his hole.

"*Oh God!*" Gabe's breath locked in his throat as his body greedily swallowed Cam's digits.

Cam grunted and pressed kisses along Gabe's quivering belly, his mouth occasionally teasing his cock while his slick fingers worked Gabe's hole, softening him, stretching him.

He pushed Gabe's right thigh up toward his chest, tugged his hip to angle him up, and pressed the tips of his fingers against a spot inside Gabe.

Stars exploded behind Gabe's eyes. A bolt of insanely intense pleasure choked his breath. He gasped for air when Cam repeated the movement, every muscle in his body twitching and tensing.

Gabe came on the fifth thrust of Cam's clever fingers, his hands fisting in the pillow under his head, his glazed eyes staring blindly at the ceiling, his mouth opening on a harsh shout, his spine arching off the bed.

CHAPTER ELEVEN

Cam bit back a groan as Gabe shattered beneath him, his cock throbbing and pulsing out cum onto his trembling belly while his hole spasmed tightly around Cam's fingers. He would never tire of this sight, of seeing this man climax from his touch. He moved his hand again, driving his fingers in and out of Gabe's body, finding his sweet spot, repeatedly rubbing and pressing against it.

Gabe's next orgasm hit him while he was still riding the waves of the first one, the sounds he made as he writhed on the bed drawing a curse from Cam's lips.

"Cam, please! I—I can't!" Gabe cried out hoarsely a moment later, shivers racking his sweat-slicked skin.

"Can't what, Gabe?" Cam said between clenched teeth.

"It's—it's too much!" Gabe panted.

"Too much what? This?" Cam dipped his head and sucked the tip of Gabe's twitching shaft, his own dick so hard it ached, his fingers still working Gabe's ass. It was so soft and wet, he knew it was ready for his cock.

"*Yes!*" Gabe sobbed, his body arching off the bed again, cum dripping continuously on his belly.

"What do you want, Gabe?" Cam said in a voice he hardly recognized. "Tell me."

Gabe shuddered at the hard, dominating tone, his dazed cobalt gaze meeting Cam's eyes.

"You! I want you inside me! *Now, goddammit!*"

Cam blinked, a choked chuckle leaving him at Gabe's barked command. He slipped his fingers out of Gabe's body, grabbed a condom from the box on the nightstand, ripped the foil open with his teeth, and sheathed himself.

Gabe watched avidly as Cam poured lube on his covered shaft and worked it in, his knees wide open and his hips undulating off the bed in anticipation of being taken.

Cam had never seen anything so sexy.

He lowered himself between Gabe's legs, propped his right elbow by the side of Gabe's left shoulder, and hooked his left hand under the back of Gabe's right thigh. He slowly pushed Gabe's leg up, his gaze locked on the man beneath him while he positioned the tip of his cock against his hole.

GABE SHIVERED AT THE FEEL OF CAM'S HEATED SHAFT against him. He stared into the heated gunmetal eyes above him and licked his lips, a sliver of apprehension washing through him and overriding the hungry ache inside his body.

Cam dropped an impossibly sweet kiss on his mouth.

"Tighten for me, Gabe. Like you did before."

He held Gabe's thigh against his chest and lowered his hand to Gabe's cock, palming him. He started stroking, his fingers slick with lube and Gabe's own cum.

Gabe shuddered and squeezed his hole, concentrating on the wicked feel of Cam's hand on his shaft. He felt himself go slack again a moment later. Cam drove Gabe's leg up higher and pushed his cock against him.

Gabe's breath hitched in his throat when the tip of Cam's shaft penetrated him. Cam kissed him as he continued gliding inside, capturing his gasps. Gabe widened his eyes at the burning sensation of his hole being stretched by the broad head of Cam's cock.

"Fuck, Gabe," Cam said between gritted teeth.

Sweat dripped off his forehead and splashed onto the corner of Gabe's mouth.

Gabe stuck out his tongue and instinctively licked it. Cam's eyes darkened above him. He leaned against Gabe's thigh, opening him wider before he flexed his hips.

Gabe moaned as Cam slid in all the way to the hilt, the sharp sting of penetration dampened by the incredible sensation of fullness in his lower body.

Cam stilled above him. He kissed Gabe again, slowly, sensuously, his cock buried deep inside him and his tongue driving Gabe crazy while his hips remained motionless. Gabe's hole spasmed and twitched around the thick shaft filling his core.

"Cam?" he said hoarsely.

"Yeah?" Cam breathed.

"I swear to God, if you don't move right—*oh fuck!*"

Gabe threw back his head and sucked air as Cam withdrew and slid in again.

"*Holy shit!*" he gasped.

A low grunt left Cam's throat as he bowed his back and started thrusting in and out of Gabe, sweat pooling and dripping from his face onto Gabe's chest.

Jolts of pleasure sparked through Gabe as Cam's cock glided inside his greedy, tight hole. Cam grabbed Gabe's right thigh and brought his lips to his left ear.

"Put these sexy legs around me, Gabe," he ordered thickly. "I've been dying to feel them on me since I first saw you."

Gabe obeyed, a whimper leaving his lips as he gripped Cam's shoulders with his hands and lifted his knees to wrap his legs around Cam's lower back, his heels coming to rest against Cam's butt cheeks.

Cam closed his hand on Gabe's right hip and tilted him up further. The angle brought his cock directly against the sweet spot inside Gabe's ass, sending white bursts of ecstasy streaming across his mind.

"*Cam!*"

Cam accelerated his pace, hips rolling hard and deep, the head of his thick shaft repeatedly stroking the place deep inside Gabe that was making him crazy, the wet sounds of their mating so arousing Gabe thought he would never tire of hearing it.

He suddenly wished there was a mirror on the ceiling. He wanted to see Cam take him. Wanted to see the man fucking him so sweetly and hotly cover his body with his own. Wanted to see the strong muscles he could feel flexing inside, above, and against him. Wanted to see his heels digging into Cam's ass as he urged him deeper. Wanted to see if they looked as good as they felt to one another. Wanted to see them come together.

The first waves of Gabe's climax wound through his body. It coiled down his spine, pooling in his cock and balls, arrowing in on his hole. Gabe cried out, his voice hoarse with pleasure, his cock jerking and splashing cum onto his belly as the mind-numbing orgasm hit him seconds later.

Cam carried on thrusting in and out of Gabe's spasming passage, gray eyes bright with passion and face flushed. It wasn't until Gabe orgasmed again that Cam grunted and bowed his head, his hips flexing erratically as he neared his own climax. He lowered his head and took Gabe's mouth in a searing kiss when he came, his harsh pants blowing out of his nose.

Gabe moaned when he felt Cam swell and pulse inside him while he was still riding the waves of his own orgasm. He instinctively tightened his hole.

"*Fuck!*" Cam cursed, gunmetal eyes darkening, cock pumping wildly into Gabe.

Gabe bit his lip while he gripped and sucked the pulsing shaft inside him with his body, prolonging

Cam's orgasm by long seconds. Cam finally collapsed against Gabe, their labored breathing the only sounds in the room. Gabe briefly closed his eyes, a ragged sigh leaving his lips, his arms and legs trembling where they wrapped around Cam.

Not only had he never felt so physically sated in his life as he did in that moment, he had never thought having sex would make him feel so emotionally content.

Cam raised his head and watched him for a silent moment, his chest still heaving, his face slick with sweat.

"That was—"

"Amazing," Gabe breathed.

Cam hesitated. "Was it really—"

Gabe kissed him before pressing their foreheads together.

"I can't believe you're even asking. My throat is sore from moaning."

Cam chuckled, the motion making his cock shift inside Gabe. Gabe groaned as his hole twitched in response.

"I think you did more than moan, Mr. Anderson," Cam said huskily.

He trailed a finger down Gabe's chest to the base of his cock.

Gabe arched an eyebrow.

"Oh, yeah? That's because you're a sex demon, Mr. Sorvino."

Cam laughed. Gabe sucked air between his teeth as pleasure darted through him from where they were still intimately connected. His eyes widened when he registered the swelling arousal stretching his insides once more.

"Ready for round two?" Cam said with a sinfully sexy grin.

He dropped a kiss on Gabe's nose and slipped out of his body with a wet sound that made Gabe blush. He stripped the used condom from his cock, discarded it, and grabbed a fresh foil.

Gabe propped himself on his elbows and stared at Cam as the latter re-sheathed and lubed himself, his own shaft stirring and swelling against his belly, his mouth drying in anticipation and a throbbing ache building deep inside his ass. He bit his lip and smiled.

I am SO screwed.

CHAPTER TWELVE

Gabe stirred and blinked. Sunlight stabbed his eyes. He squinted and raised a hand to his face before rolling away from the bright rays warming his skin. His breath stuttered in his throat as he came to rest on his left side. He froze and stared.

Cam lay sprawled on his stomach next to him, eyes closed and face relaxed in sleep, his back rising and falling lightly with his breaths. Gabe's gaze stayed locked on Cam's staggeringly handsome features for a long moment before following the lines of his powerful body to the sheet wrapped around his hips and the tantalizingly exposed curves of one naked butt cheek and thigh. Heat warmed Gabe's cheeks when he recalled how he'd repeatedly dug his heels into that tight ass only hours ago, urging Cam to drive his cock deeper inside him.

They had fucked most of the night. On the bed. On the couch. Against the wall. Gabe's pleasantly sore ass twitched as he relived all the different positions Cam had taken him in — from teaching him how to ride his cock cowboy-style to making him come repeatedly on all fours while he took him from behind. He'd even gotten his filthy wish of seeing their reflection in a mirror when Cam fucked him in the shower after Gabe went down on his knees and gave him an earth-shattering blow job.

He'd watched Cam's butt cheeks clenching and unclenching as he drove his cock in and out of Gabe's spasming hole, his powerful body supporting Gabe against the warm tiles. Gabe had been able to see his own glazed expression through the water sluicing down over their heads and bodies, his legs and arms wrapped tightly around Cam's rock-hard frame, his face twisted in pleasure, his mouth open on harsh cries as Cam brought him to one orgasm after the other.

Gabe would never forget how incredibly sexy they had looked in each other's arms.

Though a heavy weight had finally fallen from his shoulders, he could not quell the feeling of sadness that tore through his heart as he studied Cam's gorgeous face. They had only promised each other the one night. And Cam had more than delivered on his end of the bargain.

From what Gabe had gathered after listening to Ethan's words at the club and after experiencing Cam's masterful sexual prowess first hand, it was clear to him that Sorvino wasn't someone who was into relationships.

Though this was his first one-night stand, Gabe knew he was unlikely to make it a habit. The realization that he and Cam didn't want the same things in their personal lives sent a flash of regret through him. He didn't know whether he could ever find the electrifying connection he had forged with the man lying next to him with another person.

Gabe swallowed past the sudden lump in his throat and reached out to touch Cam's face. He stopped when his fingers got within a hair's breadth of Cam's lips. He fisted his hand and pulled away.

Fuck.

He needed to get out of there. Better to end this while he still had a shred of dignity left. He didn't think he could carry a normal conversation with Cam if he woke up right now. And he was pretty certain he would be unable to watch him walk away without making an ass of himself.

Gabe slipped carefully out of the bed, gathered his clothes and shoes, and went into the bathroom. He dressed hastily, wincing at his sore hips and the new sensuous ache in his lower body.

He paused at the door of the suite and cast a final glance at the man who had healed the wounds of his past. He knew he would never see him again. Although he had enjoyed his time at *Saron*, he would not go there after last night. He had too much pride to pine for Cam like a lovelorn fool.

"Thank you," Gabe whispered.

A hot feeling filled his chest, making it hard to breathe. He closed the door gently and headed for the elevator, his vision blurring.

CAM WOKE UP WITH A JOLT AT A FAINT CLICK. HE squinted drowsily at the sunlight washing through the glass wall opposite the bed and ran his fingers through his hair. His gaze dropped to the empty dent in the pillow beside him.

"Gabe?"

Cam frowned and looked toward the silent bathroom, his grogginess evaporating. His eyes widened when he registered the empty hangers where Gabe's clothes should have been.

"Shit!"

Cam leapt from the bed and ran naked to the glass wall. He looked down, his frantic gaze searching the courtyard twelve floors below. He couldn't see Gabe. He swore, dashed across the room, and yanked the suite door open.

He caught a glimpse of a dark head and a navy-blue suit as the elevator doors closed at the end of the corridor. A shocked cry reached his ears a second later.

Cam looked around and met the wild-eyed gaze of a young Japanese maid. She lowered her eyes to his groin. Color flooded her cheeks.

"I'm sorry," Cam blurted.

He slammed the door closed, yanked his clothes and shoes on, and stormed out of the suite. He stabbed impatiently at the elevator button, his gut twisting with restless agitation and his mind full of the man he had just spent the night with.

Cam's eyes widened when a wild thought came to him. He reached for his phone just as the lift arrived.

❧

GABE WALKED OUT OF THE HOTEL AND INHALED DEEPLY. The cool morning air filled his lungs, taking away some of the hotness coiled inside his chest.

The sky was a perfect blue and almost cloudless, a rare occurrence for the city. He paused and looked out to the shimmering waters of Tokyo Bay in the distance.

A smile tugged at his lips despite the sadness in his heart.

He was a changed man. One who could look forward to a future where he might one day find someone he wanted to spend the rest of his life with.

That this person would not be Cam Sorvino was something he would have to learn to live with, however bitter a pill it was to swallow.

There was a ding from his suit pocket. Gabe frowned and fished his cell out. He looked at the screen and blinked.

Who the hell—

His pulse stuttered when his brain finally registered the words staring at him from the little gray box on the white background.

When did he—

"One night is not enough!" someone shouted behind him, spelling out the message that had just sent his heart thudding against his ribs.

Gabe twisted on his heels, eyes rounding.

Cam strode across the courtyard, face flushed and gray eyes dark with an emotion that made Gabe's breath catch in his throat all over again.

"One night is not nearly goddamn enough, Gabe Anderson," Cam said in a hard voice when he reached him.

He lifted his hands to Gabe's face and took his mouth in a scorching kiss, his touch bruising, his fingers and lips communicating the urgency of the feelings running through him.

Gabe stiffened before choking back the lump in his throat. He grabbed Cam's shoulders and kissed him back just as heatedly, unheeding of the gasps around them and the people watching, hoping to similarly convey the raging storm inside his own heart. He wrapped his arms around Cam's neck, molded their bodies together, and surrendered to the man masterfully claiming his mouth.

Cam finally pulled away and pressed his lips to Gabe's forehead.

"God, I thought I was gonna have a heart attack when I woke up and you weren't there," he said hoarsely.

Gabe blinked rapidly.

"I'm—I'm sorry!" he stammered. "I thought you didn't want to—"

"Well, you thought wrong," Cam said gruffly.

He stepped back, cradled Gabe's face in his hands, and gave him a stern stare.

"Just so we're clear, what happened between us was not your average, run-of-the-mill roll in the hay. I know this might come as a shock to you, but I have never had sex like that before. Ever. You rocked my fucking world last night, Gabe Anderson. And there's no way I'm going to let this end as a one-night stand."

A thrill bolted through Gabe. He smiled tremulously before turning and pressing his lips to Cam's left palm, his confidence boosted by the incredible words the man holding him had just spoken.

"So, you're saying I'm the best man you've ever had?"

CAM GRINNED FAINTLY AT GABE'S TEASING TONE, HIS chest tight with emotion at the unspoken affirmation in the blue gaze opposite him.

"Yeah, I am."

"What about women?" Gabe murmured, his eyes sparkling.

Cam brought his lips to Gabe's left ear.

"Your ass is the best thing my cock has ever tasted, and your body is the most magnificent work of art my lips, tongue, and fingers have ever touched," he whispered hotly. "Just watching you orgasm could make me come."

Gabe's breath shuddered out of his lips, his cheeks warming with color. "God, you're such a cocktease," he groaned.

Cam grinned. He didn't have to look down to know Gabe was hard again.

"Yeah, well, get used to it. You're gonna be dating this cocktease."

Gabe blinked. "Wow. We're gonna date?"

Cam chuckled, a sudden bolt of nervousness shooting through him. "It's a first for me, so take it easy."

Gabe watched him steadily. "Okay," he said, his expression telling Cam he'd registered the anxiety behind his words. "Maybe we should lay down some ground rules, make this less demanding for you."

Cam arched an eyebrow, puzzled. "I'm listening."

"First, I think we need to stick to the five-date rule," Gabe said, deadpan.

Cam's trepidation evaporated in a flash. "No way! My dick won't last that long!"

Gabe sucked air through his teeth and shook his head with an expression of fake disappointment, blue eyes glinting while he struggled to contain the laughter clearly threatening to bubble out of him.

"Okay, this is gonna be hard for me, but I'm willing to consider the three-date rule."

Cam draped an arm around Gabe's shoulders and guided him toward the street, chest filling with contentment; it was pretty hard to believe the commitment-phobic asshole that he was had actually suggested he and Gabe start seeing each other. He didn't know what this feeling growing inside him was. Didn't want to put a name to it yet. All Cam knew was that he couldn't let go of the achingly beautiful man who had surrendered himself so sweetly to him last night.

"How about we say two hours, just enough time for us to head to this neat little place I know for breakfast?" he drawled.

Gabe sighed and lowered his head against Cam's shoulder. "You're gonna be one of those pushy arrogant boyfriends, aren't you?"

Cam chuckled. "Get used to it."

They headed leisurely down the road, basking in silent enjoyment of each other's company.

"By the way, when did you put your number in my phone?" Gabe said curiously after a while.

"When you were in the shower last night," Cam replied with a grunt. He dropped a kiss on Gabe's head. "Call it instinct, but I get the feeling you're gonna be the kind of boyfriend I'm gonna have to keep a tight leash on."

Gabe twitched before mumbling a protest.

Cam's eyes widened as he took in the rising color on Gabe's cheeks. A thrill of intuition darted through him.

"Gabe Anderson, did you just have a kinky thought?"

"I did not!"

"You did, didn't you?" Cam grinned, delight and a hot tingle of anticipation filling him. "You know, Joe still keeps some bondage stuff around at *Saron* from his days as an escort. I've always wanted to try—"

"Don't you dare!" Gabe pressed a hand to Cam's mouth, his ears bright red. "You drop this topic *right now*, Cam Sorvino!"

Cam looked at the blushing gorgeous man beside him and laughed out loud, so happy he could burst.

"Oh, this is gonna be *so* much fun!"

Gabe groaned in response.

THE END

§.

What happens when a stubborn, sexy bartender is determined to make his boss fall in love with him?

Get The Escort (Nights #2)
Turn the page to read an extract now!

THE ESCORT (NIGHTS #2) SPECIAL PREVIEW

CHAPTER ONE

JOE CAVENDISH SWALLOWED A GROAN AS HE STARED AT the tantalizing ass ten feet from him.

That little tease. I'm sure he's doing it on purpose.

"Do you have to be on your hands and knees for that?" he said with a sigh. "It's not exactly as if I'm a fucking slave driver, you know. I did just buy one of those ridiculously expensive mopping robots for the staff to use."

Ethan Skye looked over his shoulder and narrowed his eyes at Joe where the latter sat at the bar drinking a coffee.

"Your robot knows dick about oak floors. And I'm not cleaning. I'm fixing the scratch that asshole made when he dragged that metal case in here yesterday. I mean, who the fuck lugs that kind of shit around? And, FYI, his gin tasted like crap, so we're not getting it."

Joe arched an eyebrow and glanced around *Saron*'s opulent interior.

"You do realize I own the place, right?"

Ethan gave the floor a final wipe with a polishing cloth and rose to his feet.

"And I'm your best bartender. What's your point?"

He placed his toolbox on the counter and studied Joe with a haughty expression.

Joe couldn't deny the truth of his words. Although *Saron* had rapidly gained a reputation as the most exclusive gay club in Tokyo since he first opened for business four years ago, part of its phenomenal success of late had a lot to do with the stunning blond with the captivating green eyes who had waltzed into his club eleven months ago and demanded he give him a job.

It wasn't every day that someone made Joe Cavendish look at them twice. Ethan Skye had made him look twice, three times, and a dozen more after that.

That fact alone should have had Joe running hell-for-leather in the other direction. He couldn't recall the last time his body had had such an immediate, visceral reaction to a stranger, even during his years working as an escort. Still, he'd found himself unable to deny the demand in the mesmerizing green eyes that had bored so intensely into him and had reluctantly invited the young man back for an interview the week after.

Surprise had darted through Joe when Ethan had pulled out his résumé and asked if he could do the interview there and then, offering the club owner a foretaste of his bossy nature. Joe had taken the professional, double-sided sheet and studied it with a frown.

"Says here you're a Stanford business graduate."

He'd looked up into Ethan's cool expression. "Why the hell would you want to be a bartender in Shinjuku?"

"I'm not made for a city job. Besides, I almost flunked business school."

Joe had bought that cock-and-bull story about as much as he believed in Santa Claus. He'd been around the block enough times to tell when somebody was harboring secrets. After all, he had some pretty dark ones of his own.

Ethan had passed his interview with flying colors and didn't even blink when Joe challenged him to make *Saron*'s trademark cocktail and give it his own personal twist. One sip of the intoxicating drink Ethan made was all it took for Joe to realize he shouldn't let the cocky blond slip out of his hands and into a competitor's clutches.

In the months since Ethan had been at *Saron*, the bartender had become a key member of his staff. He got on with everyone, including the normally taciturn doormen, and had charmed all the patrons with his quick wit and exquisite drinks. The fact that he was goddamn easy on the eye didn't hurt either.

Had Joe known at the time the fresh hell he would be inviting into his life by giving Ethan the bartending job, he would probably have refused the young man. Joe knew a lot of the club's patrons would kill to get their hands on *Saron*'s newest bartender. Not only was Ethan drop-dead gorgeous, he had also been blessed with a naturally athletic physique; just enough muscle not to be brawny and the entire package perfectly toned in all the right places.

Places Joe had been aching to touch for months.

As days turned to weeks and weeks to months, the spark that had been there between them from the start had ignited into a maelstrom of full-blown lust that had Joe's cock aching most times he came within twenty feet of the alluring bartender.

It didn't help that he'd once walked in on Ethan in the staff changing room and gotten an eyeful of the delicious body he'd been fantasizing about. Joe had wondered for days afterward how many men had kissed the mole he'd glimpsed on Ethan's right hip, just above his low-riding briefs. And how many more had tasted his honey skin and claimed his tight ass.

The fact that Ethan wouldn't refuse Joe made their situation all the more bittersweet. He had made it abundantly clear he was gay from the first day he started working at *Saron*. And just as Joe's eyes seemed to gravitate to Ethan whenever they were in the same room, Ethan always tracked him with his heated gaze in return.

But even though Ethan had turned the carefully ordered life Joe had built over the last few years upside down and had become the source of some of Joe's filthiest fantasies, hooking up with the young man was the one thing the club owner wouldn't let happen. He'd had his fingers burned once before when he'd mixed business with pleasure, and he'd made it a rule never to do so again.

Unfortunately, Ethan didn't seem to agree with him on the clear dividing lines Joe had set from the start of their working relationship. He was constantly pushing at the boundaries, testing the limits of Joe's patience and his raging libido.

Just as he was doing right now.

"I've spoken to our regular gin supplier," Joe said with a grunt. "It seems the shortfall we're experiencing is going to last some time. We need to find another company to get our stock from." He hesitated. "Eveline can probably—"

"No!" Ethan snapped. The mere mention of the name Joe had just uttered made the bartender grit his teeth. "Give me a day. I'll get you another supplier by tomorrow."

Joe bit back a frustrated sigh at Ethan's stormy expression. He still didn't know how Ethan had discovered his connection with *Le Secret*, the internationally renowned, upscale escort service Joe used to work for before he started *Saron*. It sure as hell hadn't come from one of Joe's other staff, who knew nothing of his past.

The brainchild of Eveline Claude, a former escort and professional dominatrix, *Le Secret* catered only to the wealthiest of clientele—from politicians and royalty, to movie stars and billionaires. With clubs in five cities around the world, the business advertised itself as offering a strictly social service, even though a lot of its clients were really after sex. Eveline had always made it clear that what happened behind closed doors was a private matter between client and escort, and she'd kicked out plenty of both over the years who hadn't followed the strict rules she laid out for her clubs.

Though he was no longer in Eveline's employ, Joe still accepted the odd gig from her. After all, she was the one who had saved him from the nightmare he'd been living in when he worked in the shady underworld of New York's sex and strip clubs between the ages of fifteen and twenty-four. He also owed her big time for the loan she'd given him to set up his own business, money he'd paid back within a year of opening *Saron*'s doors.

That most people would find his background and previous lifestyle distasteful was not something that kept Joe awake at night. Yet Ethan's reaction when he'd first challenged Joe about the jobs he still took on for *Le Secret*'s owner had stung. It wasn't judgment Joe had read in Ethan's eyes that day. It was resentment and frustration that Joe could willingly sleep with a complete stranger but not lay a finger on him.

Joe considered the young man presently scowling at him; he knew not to disbelieve the words he had just spoken. Ethan had made similar promises in the past on the rare occasions Joe had been in a fix and always delivered on them. Joe narrowed his eyes.

"I'd really like to know who your source is."

The corner of Ethan's mouth lifted in an insolent smile that made Joe want to kiss him hard.

"I'm afraid I would have to kill you if I revealed that information."

A bark of laughter left Joe's lips at the threat. His groin tightened at the torrid image that flashed across his inner vision. Of Ethan slowly and sweetly killing him with his exquisite body while he straddled Joe and rode his cock, his sexy hips undulating with every hard thrust of Joe's dick while his filthy mouth opened on throaty cries and moans.

"Here, pour me another coffee."

Ethan rolled his eyes. "Yes, master."

Joe swallowed another groan.

Yup, he's doing it deliberately.

Read The Escort today

AFTERWORD

To all my friends who helped make this possible. You know who you are.

To you, my readers. Thank you for reading Gabe and Cam's story. I hope you loved this first book in the Nights series. I would be grateful if you could leave a review on Goodreads or on the store where you purchased this book. Reviews help readers like you find my books and I truly appreciate your honest opinions about my stories.

Make sure to sign up to my store newsletter for special deals on my books and new release alerts. Or you can sign up to my author newsletter instead to get upcoming release notifications, sneak peeks, and giveaways.

ABOUT THE AUTHOR

Ava Marie Salinger is the romance pen name of an Amazon bestselling author with a passion for writing addictive tales. Known for her action-packed and thrilling urban fantasy novels, she has expanded her repertoire with the introduction of the M/M urban fantasy romance series Fallen Messengers. Additionally, she has penned the scorching hot contemporary M/M romance series Nights and Twilight Falls as A.M. Salinger. When not immersed in her writing, Ava can be found curating inspiring music playlists, indulging in her love for nature, marveling at the latest gadgets, and savoring Chinese cuisine.

You can find all of Ava's books on her author store at
shop.adstarrling.com